The Wheels on the Bus

Jane Cabrera

"All aboard and off we go..."

Beep! Beep!

GULLANE
CHILDREN'S BOOKS

The wheels on the bus go round and round,
Round and round, round and round.

The wheels on the bus go round and round,
All day long!

The Lion on the bus goes

Roar, roar, roar,
Roar, roar, roar,
Roar, roar, roar.

The Lion on the bus goes

Roar, roar, roar,

All day long!

The flamingos on the bus go
Flap, flap, flap,
Flap, flap, flap,
Flap, flap, flap,
The flamingos on the bus go
Flap, flap, flap,
All day long!

The Zebra on the bus goes
Chomp, chomp, chomp,
Chomp, chomp, chomp,
Chomp, chomp, chomp.

The Zebra on the bus goes
Chomp, chomp, chomp,
All day long!

The monkeys on the bus go
Chatter, chatter, chatter,
Chatter, chatter, chatter,
Chatter, chatter, chatter.

The monkeys on the bus go
Chatter, chatter, chatter,
All day long!

The hyena on the bus goes
Ha, ha, ha,
Ho, ho, ho,
Hee, hee, hee.

The hyena on the bus goes
Ha, ho, hee,
All day long!

The crocodile on the bus goes

Snap, snap, snap,

Snap, snap, snap,

Snap, snap, snap.

The crocodile on the bus goes
Snap, Snap, Snap,
All day long!

The chameleon on the bus plays
Hide-and-seek,
Hide-and-seek, hide-and-seek.

The chameleon on the bus plays
Hide-and-seek,
All day long!

The animals on the bus say,
"Are we there yet?
Are we there yet? Are we there yet?"

The animals on the bus say,
"Are we there yet?"
All day long!

And the driver
on the bus says...

"Yes!
Come on, everyone,
Let's get off the bus.

Now it's time to...

The Wheels on the Bus